Pumpkin the hamster loves the flashing light and noisy siren on Dr KittyCat's vanbulance

Nutmeg the guinea pig always wants to help, especially when it comes to first aid

Clove loves and, NOT IN STOCK

D0176989

Dr KittyCat has a special treat in store for these little animals. But what is it? You'll have to read the story to find out!

For Rosa and Cynthia the
guinea pigs — J.C.

OXFORD
UNIVERSITY PRESS

Great Clarendon Street, Oxford OX2 6DP

Oxford University Press is a department of the University of Oxford.
It furthers the University's objective of excellence in research, scholarship,
and education by publishing worldwide in

Oxford New York

Auckland Cape Town Dar es Salaam Hong Kong Karachi
Kuala Lumpur Madrid Melbourne Mexico City Nairobi
New Delhi Shanghai Taipei Toronto

With offices in

Argentina Austria Brazil Chile Czech Republic France Greece
Guatemala Hungary Italy Japan Poland Portugal Singapore
South Korea Switzerland Thailand Turkey Ukraine Vietnam

Oxford is a registered trade mark of Oxford University Press
in the UK and in certain other countries

Text © Jane Clarke and Oxford University Press 2015
Illustrations © Oxford University Press 2015

Cover artwork: Richard Byrne
Cover photographs: Tony Campbell, Kuttelvaserova Stuchelova,
panbazil /Shutterstock.com
Inside artwork: Dynamo
All animal images from Shutterstock
With thanks to Christopher Tancock for advising on the first aid
The moral rights of the author/illustrator have been asserted
Database right Oxford University Press (maker)

First published in 2015

All rights reserved. No part of this publication may be reproduced,
stored in a retrieval system, or transmitted, in any form or by any means,
without the prior permission in writing of Oxford University Press,
or as expressly permitted by law, or under terms agreed with the appropriate
reprographics rights organization. Enquiries concerning reproduction
outside the scope of the above should be sent to the Rights Department,
Oxford University Press, at the address above

You must not circulate this book in any other binding or cover
and you must impose this same condition on any acquirer

British Library Cataloguing in Publication Data
Data available

ISBN: 978-0-19-274278-0 (paperback)

2 4 6 8 10 9 7 5 3

Printed in China

Paper used in the production of this book is a natural, recyclable product
made from wood grown in sustainable forests. The manufacturing process
conforms to the environmental regulations of the country of origin.

Dr KittyCat

is ready to rescue

Clover the Bunny

Jane Clarke

OXFORD
UNIVERSITY PRESS

Chapter One

Peanut peeped round the door of Dr KittyCat's clinic.

A queue of young fluffy animals was waiting outside. They were all twisting and turning uncomfortably and scratching at their paws. Peanut slammed the door and turned tail into the room.

'Eek!' he squeaked. 'There's an outbreak of pawpox in Thistletown!'

'Don't panic, Peanut,' Dr KittyCat meowed calmly. 'Every doctor sees lots

of cases of pawpox. Nearly everyone catches it when they're small. Didn't you have it when you were a little mouse? It's very infectious.'

'I did,' Peanut squeaked. 'It was horrid. My paws were so itchy I spent all day scratching and I couldn't sleep!' His whiskers quivered. 'I don't want to have it again.'

'You can't get pawpox twice,' Dr KittyCat reassured him. 'I caught it when I was a kitten—so neither of us will catch it again. We are both immune.'

She buttoned up her white doctor's coat and swished her stripy tail. 'Now, who's first in line to see us today?'

Peanut scampered over to his
desk and picked up Dr KittyCat's
Furry First-aid Book; then he went to
open the door. A little black kitten crept
into the clinic.

'Hello, Daisy,' Peanut greeted her.
'How can we help?'

Daisy blinked her big round eyes.

'I don't feel very well,' the kitten
snuffled. 'My legs and tail ache.'

'I'm sorry to hear
that, but you've come
to the right place,'
Peanut told her.
'Dr KittyCat's a
brilliant doctor.'

He glanced at Daisy's paws. 'That's odd,' he told Dr KittyCat. 'I don't see any spots.'

'One of the first signs of pawpox is feeling unwell and achy,' Dr KittyCat murmured, 'and the patient often has a mild fever. I need to take your temperature, Daisy.'

Peanut clicked open Dr KittyCat's flowery doctor's bag, took out the ear thermometer, and fitted it with a new hygiene cover.

He handed it to Dr KittyCat and watched as she gently inserted it into Daisy's ear and waited for the *beep, beep, beep.*

Dr KittyCat removed the thermometer and showed Peanut the reading.

'That's slightly above normal for a kitten,' he squeaked. He threw away the hygiene cover and returned the ear thermometer to Dr KittyCat's bag. Then he opened Dr Kitty Cat's *Furry First-aid Book* and wrote down Daisy's temperature in it.

'Now, Daisy,' Dr KittyCat meowed, 'let me take a closer look at your paws.'

'I'll find the surgical headlamp . . .'
said Peanut, rummaging through a chest
of drawers. 'Got it!'

He handed Dr KittyCat what
looked like a little torch on a headband.
Dr KittyCat pulled it on and clicked on
the bright light. 'You *are* a good kitten,'

she told Daisy as she examined each tiny paw in turn.

'I can see some tiny spots, Daisy,' Dr KittyCat meowed gently. 'They're very faint at the moment, but they will get bigger, I'm afraid. You definitely have pawpox.'

Daisy hung her head.

'Pawpox isn't a serious disease,' Dr KittyCat purred comfortingly. She handed Peanut the headlamp to put away. 'But the spots will get itchy as they get bigger, and they may blister. Try not to scratch them.'

'I remember how hard that is!' Peanut squeaked.

Dr KittyCat reached up a paw and took a tube from the supplies cupboard.

'This cooling gel will help soothe the itch,' she told Daisy. 'Go home and rest, and drink plenty of water. Pawpox doesn't make you feel ill for long,' she reassured the little kitten. 'You'll soon be better, and you'll never catch it again.'

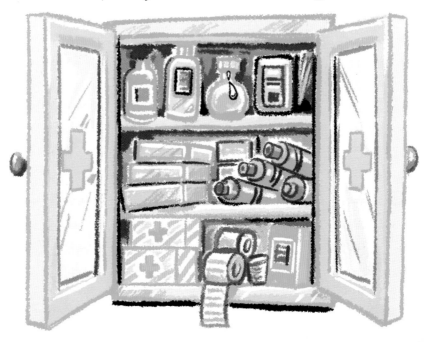

'You've been a
very good patient,'
Peanut said as he
opened the door for
Daisy to go out. 'I think

I was a
purr-fect
patient for
Dr KittyCat!

you've earned one of our
special stickers.' He handed her a round
sticker which said: 'I was a purr-fect
patient for Dr KittyCat!'

Daisy's eyes sparkled. 'I feel a bit
better already,' she purred.

It had been an extremely busy morning.

'How many cases of pawpox did I
diagnose?' Dr KittyCat asked Peanut.

Peanut checked his notes. 'Fourteen!' he squeaked.

Dr KittyCat washed her paws and settled down in a chair with a sigh. She took a ball of wool out of her flowery doctor's bag and began to click-clack away with her knitting needles.

Peanut glanced up nervously from his desk. *Oh dear,* he thought, *that's a mouse-sized scarf . . . I hope it's not for me.* Peanut wasn't always very keen on Dr KittyCat's hand-knitted things! His tail twitched as he took out his pencil and began to write up his notes in the *Furry First-aid Book.*

The old-fashioned telephone on the desk began to ring. Peanut and Dr KittyCat exchanged glances.

Brring!
Brring!

Brring!
Brring!

It could be an emergency, Peanut thought as he grabbed the handset.

'Dr KittyCat's clinic,' he said. 'How can we help you?' He listened for a moment, then put his paw over the mouthpiece.

'It's Pumpkin,' he told Dr KittyCat. 'He's heard about the outbreak of pawpox, and wants to know if we are going ahead with the camping trip later today.' Peanut glanced down at his notebook. 'Daisy, Posy the puppy, and Fennel the fox cub all have pawpox, and Sage the owlet has clawpox,' he sighed. 'So they can't come. Do you think we should cancel it?'

Dr KittyCat gazed thoughtfully out of the window. 'Pumpkin the hamster, Nutmeg the guinea pig, and Clover the bunny are fine,' she purred, 'and the sun's shining. It would be a pity to cancel . . .'

'The camping trip's on!' Peanut squeaked into the phone's mouthpiece. 'Tell the others to meet us outside the clinic. See you soon.' At the other end of the phone, he could hear Pumpkin squealing excitedly. Peanut smiled as he replaced the handset. The phone's curly cord wrapped itself around his furry little body.

'Eek!' he squeaked.

Dr KittyCat put down her knitting
and untangled him.

'Before we go, I must check the
medical supplies,' she said, opening her

flowery doctor's
bag. 'Scissors,

syringe,

medicines,

ointments, instant cool packs,
paw-cleansing gel, and
wipes,' she murmured.
'Stethoscope,
ophthalmoscope,
thermometer,
tweezers, bandages,
gauze, sticking plasters,
reward stickers . . .
and I think we should take the surgical
headlamp and magnifying glass, too.'

Peanut took them out of the drawer.
'We'll be miles away from the clinic,' he
squeaked. 'We should take

some cooling gel in case
someone comes down

with pawpox!' He
scrambled up
into the supplies
cupboard, grabbed a box

and dropped it into Dr KittyCat's bag.

Dr KittyCat squeezed her
knitting into the top of the bag
and clicked it shut.

'It's best to be prepared for
anything,' she meowed. 'First-
aiders should always be
ready to rescue!'

Chapter Two

Peanut looked up from his notes and glanced out of the window. The vanbulance was parked right outside, and the bright flowers he had painted on it were sparkling in the sunshine. Pumpkin, Nutmeg, and Clover were standing next to it, jumping up and down with excitement. They were

each carrying a backpack and a
bedding roll.

'They're here,' Peanut squeaked.
He grabbed his pencil and the *Furry
First-aid Book* and went out to join the
little animals.

'I can't wait to see inside the
vanbulance,' Clover said as he hopped
up and down while Peanut opened the
side door.

'Wow!' Nutmeg gasped excitedly.

'Wow-eee!' Pumpkin and Clover
exclaimed. 'It's great!'

The little animals piled into the van
with their backpacks and bedding rolls.

'It's got a proper table,' Pumpkin

squeaked, 'and lots of cupboards.'

'And a little kitchen with a kettle,' Nutmeg whistled.

'And lovely flowery curtains,' Clover gasped. 'But where will we all sleep?'

'This bench seat turns into Dr KittyCat's bed,' Peanut explained, 'and that's my room up there.' He pointed to a cabin just under the roof. 'I've packed tents for you three to sleep in, and we'll all eat round the campfire. It's going to be an adventure!'

'Ooh!' The little animals squealed in excitement.

Peanut pointed to the bench seat. 'Hop up here and put on your seatbelts. We'll be leaving in a minute,' he told them.

Clover took a colouring book and crayons out of his backpack and put them on the table.

'We can colour as we go along!' he said.

Nutmeg looked out of the window. 'Dr KittyCat's coming,' she squeaked.

'She's got her flowery doctor's bag with her.'

'Good,' Peanut laughed. 'We can't go without that!' He checked the animals' seatbelts were pulled tight, then he shut the door and scampered round to the front of the vanbulance.

'Everyone's safely in the back,' he called as he scrambled into the passenger seat. Dr KittyCat opened the door to the driver's side of the van, threw her flowery doctor's bag onto the floor in front of Peanut and jumped into the driver's seat.

Peanut clicked on his seatbelt and carefully curled his tail out of the way before pulling the door shut. Dr KittyCat did the same.

'Ready to roll?' Peanut squeaked.

'Ready to roll!' Nutmeg, Clover, and Pumpkin chorused from the back of the van.

Dr KittyCat turned the key. There was a *vroom, vroom, vroom,* and the vanbulance sped off.

'Put the siren on!' Nutmeg whistled.

'We can't do that in town unless it's an emergency and we're rushing to the rescue,' Peanut explained. 'And it isn't. Even though we are going really fast!' He glanced at Dr KittyCat. Her bright eyes were fixed on the way ahead, and she was smiling as she gripped the big steering wheel tightly. The vanbulance rattled over the timber bridge and headed towards Duckpond Bend.

There was a groan from the back.
'Ugh!'

'Pumpkin feels poorly!' Nutmeg and Clover yelled.

'Stop!' Peanut squeaked.

There was a *screech!* as Dr KittyCat put her foot on the brakes. As soon as the vanbulance shuddered to a halt, Peanut leaped out and rushed to open the side of the van. Pumpkin, Nutmeg, and Clover tumbled out. Pumpkin flopped onto the grass with his eyes shut tight, groaning.

Ugh!

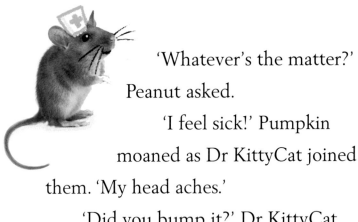

'Whatever's the matter?'
Peanut asked.

'I feel sick!' Pumpkin
moaned as Dr KittyCat joined
them. 'My head aches.'

'Did you bump it?' Dr KittyCat
asked him.

'No,' Pumpkin groaned.

'It might be pawpox!' Peanut
whispered in Dr KittyCat's ear.

'And it might not be,' she
whispered back. 'Don't panic, Peanut.'
Dr KittyCat turned to Pumpkin. 'When
did your head start to ache?' she asked.

'When I was doing some colouring
in,' Pumpkin whimpered.

'I noticed you going a bit green,' Nutmeg whistled. 'I think you're just travel-sick.'

'You're right, Nutmeg,' Dr KittyCat told the little guinea pig. 'You'd make a good doctor.'

'Thank you!' Nutmeg said, looking proud.

'Poor Pumpkin,' Dr KittyCat said comfortingly. 'Travel sickness is so horrid. Lie still for a minute,' she told him, 'and it will pass.'

Peanut jumped into the van and fetched a beaker of water.

Dr KittyCat helped Pumpkin to take little sips. She turned to Nutmeg

and Clover. 'Are you two feeling OK?'
she asked them.

They nodded their heads.

'I feel OK now, too,' Pumpkin said.

'Then we'll get back in the van and
carry on with our trip,' Dr KittyCat
meowed. 'I'll try to remember to
go more slowly.'

'I think you should shut your
eyes for the rest of the trip,' Peanut
whispered in the hamster's furry ear.

'We're not far from the campsite
now,' Dr KittyCat reassured everyone
as they set off again.

There was a little squeak from the
back seat. 'Dr KittyCat . . .' Pumpkin called.

Peanut exchanged a nervous glance with Dr KittyCat. Was Pumpkin going to be sick?

'Can you put the siren on . . . *please?'* the hamster asked.

Peanut and Dr KittyCat looked at one another and smiled. Dr KittyCat nodded.

Nee-nah! Nee-nah! Nee-nah!

'Just for a second
or two . . .' Peanut said.
Then he slammed his
paw on the button on the
dashboard that put on the flashing light
and the noisy siren.

'Yay!' Pumpkin, Nutmeg, and
Clover squealed.

At last the vanbulance bumped through
an open gate into a grassy campsite at
the edge of a wood. 'We've arrived!'
Dr KittyCat meowed. She switched off
the engine. She slid open the doors and
everyone jumped out.

Peanut looked around. 'There's a campfire pit!' he exclaimed, pointing to a circle of stones.

Nutmeg, Clover, and Pumpkin rushed to help Peanut heave three rolled-up tents out of the vanbulance. 'Make sure you put them up at a safe distance from the fire pit,' he told them.

The animals pulled out the tent poles.

'It's best to choose a flat piece of ground to pitch your tent on,' Peanut told them. They all worked together to put up the tents. Then Peanut took out a wooden mallet and went round hammering in tent pegs.

'Can I have a go?' Nutmeg asked. Peanut reluctantly handed her the rubber mallet.

'Be careful, we don't want any accidents,' he murmured, but it was too late.

'Ow!' Nutmeg squealed, jumping up and down, shaking her paw in pain.

Chapter Three

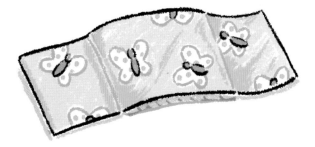

'Let me see,' Dr KittyCat said as she hurried over. Nutmeg held out her paw.

'It's just a tiny bruise,' Dr KittyCat said. 'It doesn't even need a sticking plaster.'

Nutmeg's ears drooped.

'But it wouldn't hurt to have one,' Peanut said, fetching the box. Nutmeg

grinned from ear to ear as she chose
a plaster with butterflies on it. 'Now,
who wants to come with me to collect
firewood?' Peanut asked.

'Me! Me! Me!' yelled Pumpkin,
Nutmeg, and Clover.

Dr KittyCat smiled. 'You have
plenty of helpers, Peanut,' she purred.
'I'll stay here. I have a surprise to get
ready for everyone.'

'What is it?' Peanut and the little
animals squeaked.

'It wouldn't be a surprise if I told
you!' Dr KittyCat gave them a wave
and headed towards the vanbulance.

'Stay together, everyone,' Peanut

told Nutmeg, Clover,
and Pumpkin as he led
the way down the narrow
path into the woods. 'Don't wander
off—you might get lost.'

The air was cool and still in
the woods. Bright green leaves were
beginning to burst from the
hazelnut and oak trees,
and the ground was
carpeted in a beautiful
purple haze of
bluebells. Peanut
stopped in
a grassy
clearing.

'Dead wood makes the best firewood,' he said. 'And there are lots of fallen trees around here.' He tugged at a dry branch attached to an old tree trunk. It came away in his paws with a loud *crack!*

'Ow!' Peanut exclaimed, shaking his paw. A sharp piece of wood was sticking out of it. It hurt a lot. It made his whiskers quiver.

Clover's eyes opened wide. 'That's a big splinter!' he gasped.

'I'll get it out.' Peanut gritted his teeth and pulled. But the end of the wood broke off, leaving the point buried in his paw.

'Let me look,' Nutmeg said. She
took Peanut's paw the way Dr KittyCat
had held hers and stared closely at it.
'Oh dear,' she whistled. 'You'll have to
get Dr KittyCat to take that out.'

Peanut knew she was right. 'It
shouldn't take long,' Peanut told the
other animals. 'Don't leave the clearing.
I'll be back in no time.'

He scurried down the path,
cradling his hurt paw in his good one.

'Eek!' he cried as he reached the
vanbulance. 'Dr KittyCat, I need your
help! There's a splinter in my paw!'

Dr KittyCat was blowing up a big
round paddling pool with a foot pump.

'They'll love that!' Peanut squeaked as Dr KittyCat plugged the valve. 'It's a great surprise.'

'It is, isn't it?' Dr KittyCat purred. 'Let me treat your splinter and then you can help me fill the pool with water.'

'I can't stay,' Pumpkin squeaked. 'I left Nutmeg, Pumpkin, and Clover in the woods. Please be quick!'

'Don't panic, Peanut,' Dr KittyCat said calmly. 'It won't take long to get a splinter out. Go and wash your paw carefully in warm water, while I get my things ready.' Peanut went to the little sink in

the kitchen area of the
vanbulance and soaped his
paw under running water.

'Ouch!' he squeaked. 'It's really
painful.'

Dr KittyCat followed Peanut into
the van and clicked open her flowery
doctor's bag. She put on her surgical
headlamp. 'Let me see,' she meowed.

Peanut put his paw into Dr
KittyCat's warm furry one. The splinter
was so sore his paw was shaking.

'It will stop hurting soon,' Dr
KittyCat promised. 'First, I'm going to
take a look at the splinter to see how
deep it is,' she told Peanut. 'Then I'll

know the best way to get it out.' Peanut held his breath as she carefully examined the site of the splinter.

'Good,' Dr KittyCat purred. 'I can see the end of the splinter sticking up out of the skin so I should be able to pull it out the way it went in.' She reached for her tweezers. Peanut shut his eyes.

'There!' Dr KittyCat told him. 'It's out.'

Peanut's whiskers stopped quivering. Dr KittyCat was such a brilliant doctor he hadn't even felt her removing the splinter.

'Gently wash the wound again and pat it dry,' Dr KittyCat told him. 'Then I'll put a sticking plaster over it to keep it clean.'

Peanut did as he was told. He chose a sticking plaster covered in little paw prints.

'It's almost as good as new,' he said, admiring his clean pink paw with the sticking plaster on it. He felt much better.

'Keep it clean and tell me if there's any increased soreness, redness, itching, or swelling.' Dr KittyCat said as she packed away her headlamp and tweezers. 'You were very brave, Peanut,' she purred.

Peanut felt as if he would burst with pride. Then he remembered . . . Pumpkin, Nutmeg, and Clover were waiting for him.

'I have to get back to the woods!' Peanut jumped out of the vanbulance and rushed towards the woods. What looked like two walking bundles of twigs were heading up the path.

Nutmeg and Pumpkin were carrying armfuls of firewood.

'We got lots of wood,' panted Nutmeg from behind a pile of twigs.

'Brilliant!' Peanut exclaimed. 'But, where's Clover?'

'He's not far behind us,' Pumpkin said.

Peanut stared down the narrow path that led into the woods.

'I can't see him,' he murmured.

'Waah!' A distant, shrill shriek echoed out of the woods. 'Waah! Waah!'

Peanut raced back to Dr KittyCat. 'It's Clover. He's hurt!' he squeaked. 'Ready to rescue?'

Dr KittyCat picked up her flowery doctor's bag. 'Ready to rescue!' she meowed. 'We'll be there in a whisker!'

Chapter Four

Peanut grabbed the *Furry First-aid Book* and dashed down the path after Dr KittyCat. Nutmeg and Pumpkin dropped their firewood and followed, too.

'Clover!' they all yelled. Peanut listened. Somewhere in the distance he thought he could hear a little animal sobbing. He held his breath. The grassy clearing in the wood was still and silent.

Nutmeg pointed to the entrance to a burrow. 'What if Clover's hurt and he's crawled down a rabbit hole?'

'Clover!' they called. 'Where are you?'

'Waah!' The little bunny's distress call seemed to echo all around them.

'It doesn't sound as if he's down a hole,' Peanut said. 'He's over there somewhere.'

He pointed to the edge of the clearing. 'Come on!'

Dr KittyCat, Nutmeg, Pumpkin, and Peanut raced towards Clover's cries. At the far side, there was a pile of wood near the base of an old tree trunk.

'He dropped his firewood,' Pumpkin said, worriedly. 'Something must have happened to him!'

'Waah!' Clover wailed again. Dr KittyCat's ears pricked up. Peanut glanced round wildly, but all he could see was shadows.

'I've spotted him!' Dr KittyCat exclaimed. She pointed to a little mound of fur huddled up in the dappled light. It was Clover, quivering from his whiskery nose to his cotton-wool tail.

'Waah!' Clover cried. 'Waah!'

'Dr KittyCat's come to rescue you, Clover,' Peanut squeaked. 'Everything will be all right now.'

Dr KittyCat knelt down beside the distressed bunny.

'What's wrong, Clover?' she asked him gently.

'My paws hurt!' the bunny sobbed.

'Did you fall over anything?' Dr KittyCat asked.

'No!' Clover snuffled.

'Did a branch or anything hit you on the paws—or the head?'

'No!' Clover cried.

'That's good,' Dr KittyCat meowed reassuringly. 'Can you wriggle all your paws?'

'Yes!' Clover whimpered.

'Good,' Dr KittyCat said again. She turned to Peanut. 'Clover hasn't broken anything,' Dr KittyCat told him. 'I think it's safe to move him.'

'He's been collecting firewood. Maybe he's got splinters in his paw, like me,' Peanut squeaked. 'Splinters are very painful.'

Nutmeg and Pumpkin nodded.

'I need to see your paws properly, Clover,' Dr KittyCat purred. 'Let's move you out into the sunshine.'

Clover nodded miserably as Dr KittyCat and Peanut helped him to his feet.

'Ow!' he wailed.

Dr KittyCat examined each of his paws in turn.

'You haven't got any splinters that I can see,' Dr KittyCat told Clover. 'But you do have a rash of bumps all over your paw pads that are turning into blisters. The rash is worse on your back paws than on your front paws. It must be very sore and itchy.'

'It is!' Clover wailed.

'Blisters?' Peanut opened Dr KittyCat's *Furry First-aid Book* and leafed through his notes.

'Eek!' He squeaked. 'It's pawpox.
Clover's caught pawpox! We will all
have to pack up and go home!'

Nutmeg and Pumpkin looked at
one another and burst into tears.

'No!' they cried.

Chapter Five

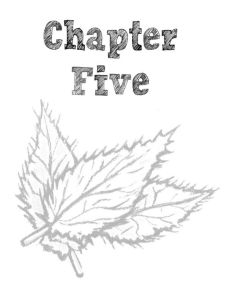

'Don't panic, Peanut,' Dr KittyCat meowed. 'It does look as if it might be pawpox, but I need to do a few more checks to make sure.'

She turned to the little bunny. 'Do you have a headache, Clover?' she asked.

Clover shook his head.

'Good,' Dr KittyCat murmured. 'Do you have any other aches and pains?'

'Only in my paws,' Clover moaned.

Dr KittyCat turned to Peanut. 'I need to check Clover's temperature,' she told him.

Peanut opened Dr KittyCat's flowery doctor's bag and passed her the ear thermometer. Dr KittyCat gently placed it in Clover's ear and waited for the *beep, beep, beep* before taking it out.

'Clover doesn't have a fever,' Dr KittyCat said slowly, showing Peanut the display on the thermometer. 'He might not have pawpox after all.'

'I really hope he doesn't,' Nutmeg whistled.

'Me, too,' agreed Pumpkin.

Peanut put the thermometer back in Dr KittyCat's bag. 'What's wrong with Clover's paws then?' he asked.

'They hurt!' the bunny squealed.

'Don't worry, Clover, we will find out what the matter is,' Dr KittyCat meowed. 'What were you doing when your paws began to hurt?'

'Collecting firewood,' Clover said between sniffs. 'I got lots!' He nodded towards the big pile of dry sticks. 'I was carrying it back to camp. But my paws hurt so much I had to drop it.'

'Maybe he has lots and lots of tiny splinters,' Peanut squeaked. He rummaged through her bag and handed Dr KittyCat her surgical headlamp. 'Would it help to use a magnifying glass?'

'Good idea!' Dr KittyCat meowed. 'Can you hold it steady for me?'

'I'll try, but my paw's still a bit sore.'
Peanut carefully heaved the big heavy
magnifying glass out from the bottom
of Dr KittyCat's bag. He clutched it in
both paws and tried not to let it wobble,
as Dr KittyCat shone her headlamp on
Clover's back foot and slowly examined
each of the bunny's little paw pads.

'I can't see any splinters,' she told
Clover. She raised her head.

'Thanks, Peanut, you've been a
great help. You can put the magnifying
glass down now.'

'Phew.' Peanut sighed with relief as
he stashed the magnifying glass and the
headlamp back in the bag.

'Close up, Clover's blisters look like clusters of wasp or bee stings, but much, much smaller,' Dr KittyCat told him.

A whole rash of teeny-tiny stings, thought Peanut. 'Did you stomp on an ants' nest, Clover?' he asked.

'I don't think so,' Clover snuffled.

'It's a bit of a puzzle,' Dr KittyCat said, 'but we will work it out. Where were you gathering firewood, Clover?'

'Over there . . .' Clover waved a paw behind him towards a patch of dark green plants that were growing among the bluebells. A bunny-sized trail of flattened leaves led through them.

Peanut scampered over to take a look. The plants were higher than his head. They had leaves with raggedy edges and, from underneath, it looked as if they were covered in tiny hairs.

'I've got it! It's not pawpox!' Peanut squeaked. 'We can stay and have our campfire after all!'

Nutmeg and Pumpkin jumped up and down squealing, 'Yay!'

'So what *is* wrong with Clover?' Nutmeg asked after a few moments.

'He's been stung!' Peanut squeaked. 'Clover has walked through a patch of stinging nettles!'

Chapter Six

'I didn't realize that I'd stepped in stinging nettles,' Clover snuffled.

'That's because you were carrying so much firewood,' Nutmeg told him. 'I couldn't see where I was going, either!'

'Poor Clover—nettle stings are horrid. No wonder your paws are so sore,' Dr KittyCat meowed. 'Luckily, I

have something that will relieve
the pain.'

She took out a tube of gel and
soothed it on Clover's blistery rash.

Clover sighed with relief. 'That
feels lovely and cool,' he said.

'The sting will slowly fade away,'
Dr KittyCat promised.

'It's fading a bit already.' Clover smiled a wobbly smile.

'You are a very brave bunny,' Dr KittyCat purred. 'I have one of my special stickers for you in my bag.'

'Thanks!' Clover's eyes lit up as Dr KittyCat patted the sticker onto the little bunny's jumper.

'Can I have one?' Nutmeg whistled. *'Please?* I bruised my paw and you looked at it.'

'And me!' Pumpkin squeaked. 'I was travel-sick!'

I was a purr-fect patient for Dr KittyCat!

Peanut glanced at his sore paw.
'I had a nasty splinter,' he squeaked.
'Please may I have a sticker, too?'

'Of course!' Dr KittyCat smiled as
they all stuck their stickers on. 'Now, let's
take the firewood back to the campsite,'
she meowed. 'My surprise is waiting and
I need some help to fill it up.'

'A paddling pool! Yay!' The little
animals squealed in surprise and
excitement when they saw it. But Dr
KittyCat's stripy tail drooped.

'Oh no!' she meowed. 'It's gone
down! It must have a leak.'

'Don't panic, Dr KittyCat!' Peanut told her. 'It's nothing that a mouse and a box of sticking plasters can't mend!'

He checked the pool over carefully.

'It has a splinter, too,' he laughed, pulling out a piece of sharp wood.

Nutmeg, Pumpkin, and Clover heaped up the firewood in the campfire pit while Peanut stuck sticking plasters over the hole in the paddling pool. Dr KittyCat used the foot pump to blow it up again.

'It's as good as new,' she declared.

They all took turns filling it with buckets of water from the campsite tap. Then Peanut and the little animals jumped in.

Splash!

'This is making my paws feel much better!' Clover laughed as he and his friends sploshed in the cool refreshing water.

Soon, it was time to dry off their feet and light the campfire. Peanut fetched two folding chairs from the vanbulance, and Dr KittyCat settled into one and took out her knitting.

'I've nearly finished this scarf,' she purred.

'Who's it for?' Peanut squeaked nervously.

'I haven't decided yet,' Dr KittyCat meowed. Flames crackled as they all joined in the campfire songs. As darkness fell, the fire died away to just a glow.

Peanut went back into the vanbulance and found a packet of marshmallows to toast. Nutmeg, Clover, and Pumpkin rushed to find sticks to thread them onto.

'Be careful—don't burn yourselves' he begged as the little animals held their marshmallow sticks over the remains of the fire.

'Yum!' Nutmeg whistled.

'Yummy!' Clover and Pumpkin agreed.

Dr KittyCat cast off the last stitch on the scarf she was making and popped it into her flowery doctor's bag. 'Clover's already forgotten about his nettle stings,' she meowed.

'Look at him—he's covered in sticky marshmallow from nose to toes!'

'And Pumpkin's forgotten all about being travel-sick, and Nutmeg's forgotten about hitting her paw,' Peanut laughed. 'They're all having a wonderful time!'

'Everything's purr-fect now!' Dr KittyCat agreed.

There was a sudden loud
wheep! and Nutmeg leaped to
her feet.

'Something bit me!' Nutmeg
whistled.

'And me!' Pumpkin yelled.

'And me!' Clover glanced wildly
round him. 'We're sitting on an ants'
nest!' he squealed.

The little animals formed a line to see
Dr KittyCat.

'This cooling gel is very useful,' Dr
KittyCat meowed as she treated the ant
bites and gave out more stickers.

'Your stickers make everyone feel better, too,' Peanut laughed.

'Bedtime,' Dr KittyCat yawned as she closed her flowery doctor's bag. Clover, Nutmeg, and Pumpkin hopped off happily to their tents.

Peanut fetched a bucket and poured water from the paddling pool over the glowing twigs until the hissing stopped and the campfire was safely out. Then he went from tent to tent, listening to the rumbling sounds of small animal snores.

'They're all fast asleep,' he confirmed.

Dr KittyCat opened the door to the vanbulance. Peanut scampered up into his little cabin as Dr KittyCat unfolded her bed.

'That was a very eventful day,' she meowed, snuggling under her duvet. 'I was thinking we could have a treasure hunt tomorrow?'

'Great idea!' said Peanut sleepily. 'As long as it doesn't involve going through any nettle patches or ants' nests! Goodnight, Dr KittyCat!'

'Goodnight, Peanut!' yawned Dr KittyCat.

The end

What's in Dr KittyCat's bag?

Here are just some of the things that Dr KittyCat always carries in her flowery doctor's bag.

Surgical headlamp

Dr KittyCat's surgical headlamp is battery-powered so that she can take it anywhere. She wears it on her head and is able to direct the bright adjustable spotlight to examine even the smallest cut, wound, or rash.

Ear thermometer

Dr KittyCat uses her ear thermometer to see if a patient has a higher than normal temperature. This is also called a fever. She knows when to look at the reading because the thermometer makes a beeping sound when it's ready.

Tweezers

Dr KittyCat finds tweezers very handy for removing splinters but she also uses them for cleaning grazes or cuts by carefully removing specks of dirt from the wound. Dr KittyCat sterilizes her tweezers after each time she uses them.

Cleansing wipes

Cleansing wipes are individually wrapped and are moistened with sterile water. They are a very gentle way of washing an area to prevent the spread of germs. They do not contain any perfumes or chemicals that might irritate the skin of Dr KittyCat's patients.

If you loved Clover the Bunny, here's an extract from another Dr KittyCat adventure:

Dr KittyCat is ready to rescue: Posy the Puppy

This time Dr KittyCat is helping a little puppy called Posy who's worried she won't be well enough to take part in the Paws and Prizes sports day . . .

'I'll go in and keep her calm while we both figure out the best way to treat her and get her out,' Peanut suggested.

'Good idea,' said Dr KittyCat. 'Take a cool pack with you.' She opened her flowery doctor's bag.

'Oooh!' The curious crowd pushed forward to get a better look.

Peanut scurried into the tunnel.

There was just enough sunlight shining through the tough canvas for him to make out a bundle of quivering golden fur. The fluffy little puppy was curled up in a tight ball in the gloom.

'I'm here now, Posy,' he murmured.

A rubbery nose poked out of the fur ball. 'Ow!' she yelped.

Here are some other stories that we think you'll love!